BROTHER WARS

By Steven K. Smith

MyBoys3 Press

For more information, contact us at:

MyBoys3 Press, P.O. Box 2555, Midlothian, VA 23113

www.myboys3.com

Second Printing, 2018

ISBN: 978-0-9861473-2-6

To Alicia,
For loving your big brother long before
he wised up and treasured you

BROTHER WARS

CHAPTER ONE

Hi. My name is Harry.

If you're anything like me, you'll probably agree that life is pretty awesome. Most of the time, being a kid has a lot going for it. We get summer vacations, don't have to pay taxes, have free room and board, and have a constantly stocked refrigerator. Sure, we have to deal with school, chores, and a bedtime that I still think is *way* too early, but overall it's not so bad.

I do have one big problem though.

His name is Randy.

It would be bad enough if Randy were some annoying bully that lived down the block. Or if he were a huge, black dog that tried to attack me on my way to the bus stop each morning. (Yikes, that actually sounds pretty bad!)

But Randy lives in my house. We also happen to have the same parents. Yep, you guessed it, he's my big brother.

Randy and I don't get along sometimes. Actually, most of the time. I keep asking my parents if one of us was adopted, but they always say no. I still have my suspicions. Mom says things will get better as we get older, but I'm ten now, and in fourth grade, which is pretty big. Unless you have an older brother who is thirteen and kind of a bully. Then it's not so big. It's mostly just hard.

Sometimes I wonder if I did something when I was younger to make him really mad. Mom says she can't remember anything like that. She says sometimes that's just how older brothers are, but I'm not so sure. I tried to ask him once if he had mistaken me for someone else, but he just told me to shut up. He's not very nice.

Every day living with Randy is a new battle, like how soldiers never know where the enemy might be lurking or if they might step on a land mine. Randy's a human land mine. When he's out there roaming free, there's no telling when he will move in for the kill.

I'm not sure if I'm winning or losing. Every once in a while I pull out a minor victory, but who knows how long I can last under the pressure. Mom says the more years that go by, the less important our ages will be.

That's encouraging, but I just hope I can make it that far. Most of the time it feels like I'm under attack in my own house, which, as you can imagine, isn't very fun.

It's kind of like being in a war.

A brother war.

CHAPTER TWO

For whatever reason, Randy thinks it is absolutely hilarious to play jokes on people.

And when I say people, I mean me.

Like the time he locked me in the basement—which wouldn't be so bad if it was one of those cushy basements with thick carpet, a pool table, a wraparound couch, and video games on a big-screen TV. I could probably survive for months in a place like that. Longer, if it had a mini refrigerator and a microwave to make popcorn.

But my basement doesn't have a microwave or a pool table. It doesn't even have carpet. It just has a cold cement floor and cinder-block walls. There's not really anything down there. Nothing fun, at least. Just piles of boxes filled with my dad's old junk, the washing machine, and the furnace.

The worst part about my basement was that it used to have only one light switch at the top of the stairs in the kitchen. If someone (like Randy) locked someone else (like me) down there and turned out the light, it was dark. Really dark.

Pitch-black dark.

And I don't like the dark. Now I'm not talking about the regular dark, the kind when you turn the lights out at night in your bedroom. I mean extreme dark. The kind when there is no light. At all. Like in a cave. Or underwater. Or in my basement behind the furnace. Most kids don't like the dark, but I really hate it.

But I'm going too fast. You need to understand how things began. It really started at school in art class.

I was sitting next to my best friend, Nixon, like always. Our teacher, Ms. Stitch, said we needed to make a drawing of something that seemed out of place.

"What are you going to draw?" I asked Nixon.

"I'm not sure yet," he answered. "Maybe a football player on a baseball field. That's out of place, right?"

"Sure," I said, nodding my head. I thought that sounded pretty basic, but I wasn't going to tell Nixon that. Mom is always reminding me it's better to keep things to myself if they're not nice, which isn't easy.

Nixon moved his head sideways to peek at my paper. "What are *you* drawing?"

My mouth turned into a smile a mile wide. I had been hoping he'd ask me, because, well, my idea was pretty awesome.

"It's a duck," I answered proudly.

"A duck?" said Nixon.

"Yep."

"How is that out of place?" he asked.

"Well, it's not just *any* duck."

"It's not?"

"Nope," I said, trying to build anticipation. "It's a duck at a bowling alley."

I leaned back in my chair and waited for him to clap or maybe pat me on the back out of sheer admiration for my clever idea.

"Oh," Nixon said instead. "That's kind of weird."

I frowned. "It's not weird, Nixon. It's *unusual*. Ms. Stitch said to draw something out of place. Have you ever seen a duck at a bowling alley?"

He shook his head. "No."

"Well all right then."

I turned back to my paper and tried to ignore him. Nixon may be my best friend and all, but sometimes I think he needs to expand his imagination.

I'm not sure why I picked a duck at a bowling alley, but you have to admit, it does seem out of place. Ms. Stitch is always telling me I should use some of my untapped potential (which is a good thing, I think), and I figured my duck was a perfect place to start.

CHAPTER THREE

Despite Nixon's lack of enthusiasm, I really liked my picture. After school, I raced home and showed it to my mom. She said it showed some real creativity. I knew she'd understand.

Thankfully, Randy wasn't in the room, because he has something mean to say about almost everything I say or do. He was too busy talking to Marcy Hawkins on the way home from the bus stop. She lives two houses down from us, and he's always trying to act like a big man in front of her because he thinks she's pretty. Since her younger brother is my friend Nixon, I happen to know that Marcy likes Tony Morehouse and couldn't care less about Randy.

But I wasn't going to tell him that. I'm not stupid.

So after I showed Mom my art project, I was eating a snack when Randy came storming through the door.

He threw his backpack on the ground and gave me a sour look. I was pretty sure that I hadn't done anything, but I knew to keep my distance when he was in a bad mood.

For some reason, Randy liked to take his frustrations out on me. Mom kept telling him he should be looking out for me, since I'm his younger brother and all, but it never really seemed to sink in.

"What are you looking at, Frog Legs?"

I don't know why he called me that. Well, I guess it could be because sometimes when I run my legs poke out to the sides like a frog, but I can't help that. Maybe if he was nicer to me, Marcy would notice and then start to like him. That might put him in a better mood.

Maybe.

"Nothing," I answered, keeping my head down.

I stared at my granola bar. Avoiding eye contact was usually best when Randy was in a bad mood. Or a good mood, actually. Just avoiding Randy in general was usually the best plan.

Randy pulled a soda bottle out of the refrigerator and poured himself a glass.

"Mom isn't going to like you drinking soda before dinner," I said, without thinking.

As soon as I had said it, I knew I should have kept my mouth shut, but it was true. Soda has a lot of calories, it says it right there on the label. Mom was always getting mad at him for having sugary things before dinner.

"Mind your own business, Frog."

Uh-oh. That was worse than Frog Legs. Marcy must have dumped him. Although, if they weren't going out, he couldn't really be dumped, could he? I was planning on avoiding girls forever because of confusing stuff like that.

"Where's Mom?" Randy asked, glass of soda in hand, ready to chug it down.

"Um, I think she's out in the garden," I guessed, since the rose garden is where she spends a lot of her free time. It's her special place where she isn't to be bothered unless there is an extreme emergency. I'd tried to explain to her once that when you have an older brother like Randy, life could be on the verge of an extreme emergency at any moment, but I don't think she believed me.

Every year, she enters her best rose into a competition at the state fair. Last year, she won third place out of more than a hundred entries, so she was pretty psyched. This year, she's told everyone that she's going for the blue ribbon. I think that's first place.

I leaned back in my chair. At that moment, Mom was all the way back by the woods, dumping a bunch of weeds into the compost pile. I tried to calculate if I'd have a better chance of reaching her with my legs or my scream.

"What have we here?" said Randy with a chuckle, placing his now empty cup on the table.

I spun around to see my art project in Randy's hands and both of them moving toward the hallway.

CHAPTER FOUR

"Hey!" I shouted. "Put it down!"

I jumped out of my chair and ran toward him. Nobody was going to mess with my duck.

Randy smiled wide, a sinister gleam in his eye. He held the drawing high above his head with one hand while opening the door to the basement with the other.

"Don't, Randy. That's not funny," I protested. "I worked hard on that."

That was probably the worst thing to say. In all his life, I don't think Randy's ever done what I asked him to. I would have been better off telling him to tear it up and toss it down the stairs.

"What kind of *freak* draws a picture of a duck at a bowling alley?" Randy taunted. "You should have drawn a frog, Frog Legs!"

"Give it back!" I yelled.

"Sure, here you go."

He bent down as if to hand me the paper, but then in one quick motion, he turned and launched it through the doorway and down the basement stairs.

"N-O-O-O-O!" I shouted, lunging at the drawing.

I don't know how I must have looked from Randy's point of view, but to me, it was like one of those slow-motion commercials where the guy's voice trails off and he moves at half speed.

I leaped down three steps with my hand outstretched, but the paper was just beyond my reach. I banged into the wall and watched my drawing sail down the stairs, disappearing past a pile of laundry on the concrete floor below.

"Randy, I'm going to—" I started to say, turning back to the doorway.

Right then, I realized my mistake.

"Nighty night!" cackled Randy at the top of the stairs.

He slammed the door shut and locked it.

"Randy!" I yelled, banging on the door with my fist.

He flicked the lights on and off a few times, but then ultimately left them on.

"It's not my fault Marcy Hawkins thinks you're a *loser*!" I shouted at the closed door. "She must be the smartest girl in the whole school!"

That would teach him.

CHAPTER FIVE

I sat down on the step, glad the lights were still on but knowing better than to expect him to unlock the door. He was never going to let me out until Mom made him. That probably wouldn't be until dinnertime or whenever she had to check the laundry. And it was Friday, so we would be eating dinner late since Dad worked extra long on Fridays.

"This is just great," I muttered, rubbing my hand that was still sore from banging so hard on the door.

I hated the basement. It was creepy. The only light was a bare bulb over the washing machine, making everything seem mostly dark, hard, and cold. There were spiders and cobwebs and who knows what else lurking in every corner. I tried to stay out of there as much as possible. One of our chores around the house was to help bring the laundry up and down the stairs.

Right now it was Randy's job, but he kept threatening to convince Mom to switch it to me if I didn't do what he told me.

I moved down the steps, grasping the handrail tightly. My art project was nowhere to be seen. It was like the basement had swallowed it up and sucked it down into the concrete. All I could see from my perch on the bottom step was our old, iron furnace. My drawing had vanished.

The furnace was a terrible thing. It scared me most of all. In the winter, when the heat was on, it boiled and burned. Randy once told me that we used to have another brother in our family, but he got too close to the furnace, and it reached out and gobbled him up.

Of course, I didn't believe that. Not really. Though at times like this, it certainly felt possible.

The furnace looked like it could withstand a direct hit from a missile. If I had to guess, I'd say that it was made up of parts of an old army tank. Dad said that it burned at over one thousand degrees. That's hot.

I left the bottom step, cautiously moving my bare feet across the cement floor and toward the furnace. It was the only place left for my art project to be hiding. I circled around the thing like I would a wild beast. If Randy hadn't been kidding about it gobbling up children, I didn't want to find out the hard way.

When I rounded the far edge of the furnace, I spied a beige sheet of paper propped up against the cinder-block wall. My drawing! It was directly behind the furnace, but thankfully it was a warm day, so the furnace wasn't running to heat the house. Instead it sat there, cold and quiet, like a junkyard dog sleeping at the end of its chain.

I stepped carefully, as if a wrong move would wake the beast from its slumber. One foot at a time, I maneuvered behind the furnace, stretching my arm out as far as it could go until I felt the paper with my fingertip.

Got it! That wasn't so bad.

"Don't worry, I found my drawing!" I yelled up at the ceiling. I didn't want my brother thinking he could keep me down.

That was when the lights went out.

"Randy!" I screamed, my heart beating faster. I froze, waiting for him to turn the lights back on.

It was dark.

Pitch-black dark.

CHAPTER SIX

For a moment, I thought my eyes were closed. I blinked hard but couldn't tell the difference between what I saw with my eyes shut and my eyes open.

Whoever the genius was that built our house, they hadn't put any windows down there. Not even those tiny little ones that some people have up near the basement ceiling. I might as well have been two hundred feet underground in one of those naturally occurring caverns. Or buried alive in a tomb.

I gulped and tried not to think about that.

I'd borrowed a book from the library one time about a man who'd been exploring a cave out in the desert. He'd crawled into a hole that he thought led into another cavern, but the farther he went, the tighter the hole became. Before he knew it, he was wedged in so tight against the rock that he couldn't move.

I don't know what happened after that. I'd been too scared to finish the book. I told Mom about it, and she said she couldn't understand why they'd have a book like that in the library for elementary students. I agree, but I wasn't going to complain to our librarian, Mrs. Mancheesy, about it, or someone might call me a wimp. I do have a reputation to consider, after all.

I was still holding my picture, but I was wedged behind the furnace and not sure which way was out. In the dark, the space seemed smaller. The fit seemed tighter. This could be the end. I was sure of it. I may never get out of this basement.

All because of Randy.

Something weird happens when you sit long enough in the pitch-black dark. In the regular dark, your eyes start to adjust after a few minutes and you can sort of see things.

But not in the pitch-black dark. When it's pitch black, there is no light to see anything at all. You only see things from your imagination, which is probably worse. Especially when you're stuck behind the furnace in my basement.

I lifted a foot to move, but my knee clanged on a heating pipe.

"Ouch!" It was hot. Which was weird, because the furnace wasn't on.

That was when I heard it.

The low rumble of a growl. Like a wild animal was there with me in the pitch-black dark. It sounded like a monster, hissing and groaning. An iron monster.

The furnace was coming on!

I pictured Randy upstairs at the thermostat, cranking the heat up just to scare me. Well, it was working.

I grabbed my art project and blindly shuffled, stepped, and jumped my way through the dark and out from behind the furnace. It growled and belched and roared to life through the darkness, as if angry that I'd escaped. Two glowing red spots, like eyes, formed at the furnace door. I stared at them, horrified. They were calling to me, beckoning me toward the iron monster.

I couldn't tell if my eyes were playing tricks or if the furnace really had come to life. I'd always half suspected that Randy wasn't lying about sending that other brother to his doom. Maybe he and the furnace were working together, part of some terrible plan to rid the world of all younger brothers.

I'm not sure why, but there was something about those glowing eyes that I couldn't look away from. Before I knew it, I was standing right in front of the monster. I was so close I could reach out and touch it. Its beady, red eyes stared right through my head. I imagined bursts of flame licking out toward me, knocking me down to the concrete. I could barely stand the force of the heat that was pushing against my face. It was suffocating, but I couldn't look away.

CHAPTER SEVEN

I stood there, staring horrified into the face of the fiery furnace. Images of my short life started flashing before my eyes.

I was too young to die!

I remembered one night when we'd been sleeping at my grandparents' house. Randy and I had to share a bed, a pullout mattress from the couch, and it wasn't very pleasant for me. Mostly because Randy laid claim to at least two-thirds of the bed since he was bigger than me, which left me huddled on the edge of the mattress with barely any covers, poised to roll right onto the floor. I tried to complain, but he told me to shut up.

And then there was Rosco. That's my grandma's big white dog. He's a labradoodle—you know, the kind that keeps you from sneezing. Every time he'd come into the room at night, he'd walk over and lick my face because it was so close to the edge of the mattress. It wasn't fun.

But while we were lying there on the pullout, Randy told me a story about how they cook frogs. I thought he was crazy, since who would ever want to eat a frog, but he swore that in some places, frog legs were considered a delicacy.

He said you couldn't just drop a frog into a pot of boiling water like you do a lobster, since frogs can jump out before you get the lid on. But, and here's the sick part, he said if you set a frog into a pot of cold water, and then gradually turn the heat up bit by bit, the frog will boil to death without jumping out. It won't notice the temperature change until it is too late.

Randy had cackled devilishly as he told me the end of the story. I had a hard time sleeping after hearing that story because somehow I felt like he was talking about me and my nickname, but also because of Rosco. Dogs' tongues tickle.

Staring at the glowing red furnace made me feel like I was in that boiling pot on the stove. Me, Frog Legs—I mean, Harry—not knowing that I was meeting my doom until it was too late.

Maybe it was already happening. Was I already too close to the furnace? Maybe my blood was about to boil and my skin would peel away like a snakeskin. Maybe—

"Harry, are you down there?"

Unexpectedly, the basement lights flashed on, blinding me. I squeezed my eyes shut at the brightness, backing away from the furnace. The door to the basement had opened, and I heard my mom's voice.

"What in the world is going on here, boys? Randy, did you turn the heat on in the house? It's a hundred degrees in here. What are you thinking?"

I snapped back to reality, my eyes slowly adjusting. I looked up. The furnace was sitting there, innocently, like nothing had happened. The glowing eyes were gone. It looked like any other machine.

I stood, rubbing my eyes. Beads of sweat were dripping down my forehead.

"Harry?" Mom called again.

"Yes," I managed to say, still dazed.

"What are you doing down there in the dark? Come up here! Your father will be home soon and dinner's almost ready. Stop messing around with your brother."

"Coming," I answered meekly.

I slowly backed up the stairs, clutching my duck picture to my chest like it would somehow protect me, but still afraid to take my eyes off the furnace until I was safely out of the room.

CHAPTER EIGHT

All through dinner that night, Randy couldn't stop chuckling between bites of food. Dad had to keep telling him to be quiet. I tried to shoot laser beams at his forehead with my eyes, but it didn't work. I'd been lucky to save my art project, but there was no telling when Randy might try to mess with me again. If only I *could* develop a laser stare.

That night, I kept the light on in my closet. It wouldn't have been pitch-black dark in my room, but I didn't want it dark at all. I'd had enough dark.

I tried to think of how I could get back at Randy. Why did he have to be so mean? It wasn't my fault that Marcy didn't like him. What had I ever done to him besides being born into the same family?

Don't get me wrong, I love my family, but sometimes I wish Randy wasn't part of it. Nixon told me that his house was completely different. He said that Marcy was usually nice to him, she helped him with his homework, made him dinner when her parents were away, and even played board games with him on the weekend if it was raining.

At first, I didn't believe him.

"You mean she doesn't ever try to beat you up?" I asked.

He shook his head. "Never."

"Does she steal your stuff and break it on purpose?"

"Nope."

"Make up lies about things you didn't really do to get you in trouble with your mom and dad?" Surely she had to do *something*.

Nixon shook his head again. "I told you, Marcy's pretty nice. I like having her as a big sister."

I couldn't imagine actually *wanting* to have Randy as a big brother. Maybe I could swap him out with someone else. It was too late to suggest it with Nixon—he'd never go for it, since he already knew how awful Randy was—but maybe someone else at school would be more gullible.

I lay in my bed that night, trying not to think about the dark, about the furnace, tight caves, or frogs in boiling water, but it wasn't working. The more I tried *not* to think about it, the more those thoughts crept into my mind.

Mom always told me to think about a field of white snow when I was trying to fall asleep. She thought it helped, kind of like counting sheep. Those things never seemed to work for me, but I guessed it couldn't hurt to keep trying.

I was halfway through picturing a snowy field when I had an idea—a way to get back at Randy. And as I drifted off to sleep, I knew what I would do.

CHAPTER NINE

I wanted to teach Randy a lesson and make him realize he couldn't just bully me around whenever he liked. I didn't really want to hurt him (well, not much), just scare him a little bit.

Over the weekend, I worked through the plan in my head. I had to be realistic. Randy was a lot bigger than me, so I wouldn't be able to beat him up or force him into doing something he didn't want to do.

Dad had told me one time that if I couldn't work harder, then I had to work smarter. So that was what I was trying to do. Maybe this was another way of using my untapped potential. And if I could pull it off, it might just take care of Randy, once and for all.

On Monday morning, I got on the bus and sat with Nixon as usual. "I need your help," I announced.

"With what?" asked Nixon.

I told him about the incident with my duck drawing and how Randy had locked me in the basement in the pitch-black dark with the furnace.

"That's messed up," said Nixon.

"I know, that's why I need your help," I explained. I walked him through my secret plan, and he agreed to help like I figured he would. Nixon disliked Randy almost as much as I did.

I turned around in my seat and watched Randy at the back of the bus. Even though we went to different schools, my elementary school shared a bus for our neighborhood with Randy's middle school. The fact that he sat in the back and I sat in the front was the only thing that made getting to school manageable. It was good to have at least a five-seat buffer zone between us.

Maybe I could find a way to create that at home—a force field that wouldn't let Randy get within ten feet of me, like two magnets pushing against each other. That would be perfect, although I doubted anyone had invented the technology to make it happen. Maybe that could be another use for my untapped potential, but I tried not to get ahead of myself. One mission at a time.

I made Nixon promise not to tell anyone about my plan against Randy, not even Marcy, who was indirectly involved too. I needed her to say a few small things to

Nixon, although she wouldn't really know why. Nixon thought she'd be happy to play along if we told her, but I said no. I couldn't take any chances that she would warn Randy.

My life depended on keeping the plan secret. If it didn't work, or if Randy found out about it, things would probably get ten times worse with him.

But I tried not to think about that.

Failure was not an option.

CHAPTER TEN

That night, I set my alarm clock so I'd have some extra time to get ready. When I got up the next morning, Randy was still asleep, Dad was away on an overnight business trip to Chicago, and Mom was in the shower. That gave me about fifteen minutes.

I slid a box of supplies out from underneath my bed and carried it down the hallway to the basement door. I peered down the stairs through the partly open door. I couldn't see it, but I could sense the furnace there, waiting to pull me back into the pitch-black dark.

For a moment, I stood there, second-guessing the whole plan. Maybe I should just forget it.

Not this time, I decided. It was Randy's turn to be scared.

Dad's old video camera was the first thing I took out of my box of supplies. It was the kind with little tape cartridges the size of matchbox cars. He told me once that before everyone had cell phones, these were what people used to take videos. Pretty weird.

I plugged the power cord into the wall and then into the camera before switching it to *night mode* so it could record in the dark. I turned off the lights to make sure it was working. It was actually cool. If I strapped it to my head, I'd be able to see like one of those Navy SEALs with night vision goggles. Sort of.

I placed the camera on a shelf at the top of the stairs, positioning the lens to point down into the basement. I hoped the little bits of light that snuck into the basement around the door would give the camera enough light to see what was going on. Satisfied with the positioning, I turned the camera off. I would press record later, when the time was right.

Next, I took two walkie-talkies from the box, setting them both to *channel 1*. I'd replaced the batteries the night before to make sure they were ready to go. I hid one behind a pile of laundry next to the washing machine. The other unit went in my pocket.

I eyed the furnace warily as I walked past, but it seemed to be sleeping. Without Randy turning the heat up, it seemed pretty safe, but you can't be too careful.

CHAPTER ELEVEN

The last item in the box was a love letter.

No, not a real one. That would be gross. It was a fake note that I'd written to Randy from Marcy in big, girly letters. Nixon had borrowed his sister's notebook so we could copy her handwriting. It was a pretty good fake, if I did say so. But I also figured Randy would be too distracted by a note from Marcy to analyze it very carefully.

I stuck the note in my other pocket and stashed the empty box under the stairs. I reached the kitchen just as Mom was coming down the hallway.

"Morning, Mom," I said, smiling and trying to play it cool.

"Good morning, Harry. Can you go tell your brother that it's time to wake up? I swear he'd sleep all day long if I let him."

"Sure, Mom," I answered.

Perfect. I needed an opportunity to get the note into his backpack. Here was my chance.

Before waking up Sleeping Beauty, I dropped the second walkie-talkie into my backpack and then stopped at my parents' room. A quick spray of Mom's perfume gave the love letter a finishing touch.

I tiptoed over to Randy's room, peeking my head through the door. Sure enough, his dark form lurked beneath the covers. I spotted his backpack propped up against the wall and under a pair of shorts.

Carefully, I inched over and unzipped the front pocket. I was nearly silent, but Randy let out a big snore. He rolled over in his bed so that his face was turned toward me. I froze, trying to blend into the shadows. I was hoping he was just shifting in his sleep, but he let out a big sigh and started kicking at the sheets.

Unbelievable!

Randy never woke up on his own without Mom having to bother him. I tried to make myself look like a piece of furniture as Randy sat up and stretched. He was facing my direction, but his eyes were still closed. He stood and grunted, scratching under his arms like a monkey.

Normally that would have been hilarious, but

frozen where I was, the sight was terrifying. He was only two feet away from me when he turned and walked into the bathroom.

Whew! That was a close one.

I dropped the note into his backpack, quickly zipping the pocket back up.

I'd crossed the point of no return.

The trap was set.

Now I just had to wait for Randy to take the bait.

CHAPTER TWELVE

We made it through breakfast and onto the bus like normal.

"Did you do it?" Nixon asked me, once Randy had passed us down the aisle.

I nodded excitedly. "The deed is done."

Nixon looked a little nervous. "Are you sure this is a good idea? I mean, what if Randy finds out and then comes after us?"

I rolled my eyes. "It's fine," I said. "What could possibly go wrong?"

The truth was that I was a little worried about that too, but I kept reminding myself about the basement. If I didn't stand up for myself now, I might have to live with this sort of torture for the rest of my life.

"A lot of things," said Nixon, glancing over his shoulder at Randy in the backseat. "*You* have no choice but to put up with him, since you're his brother, but I'm just an innocent bystander. There's no reason to get me involved."

"Trust me," I said, trying to sound confident. "My plan is foolproof. It has to work."

At least, I hoped what I was saying was true. Sure, there were plenty of things that could go wrong, but I had a good feeling about it.

"Okay…" Nixon said, not sounding too convinced. "I hope you're right."

I kept working through my plan all day. I'd trusted that Randy wouldn't find the note in his backpack until he got to class and reached for his books. Then, if things worked right, he'd read the love letter and follow its simple instructions. It said that Marcy couldn't hide her feelings for Randy any longer. That she was madly in love with him and wanted to meet at his house after school.

Of course, all that was utterly ridiculous. I was counting on Randy not being the brightest kid in the world. Honestly, I wasn't sure how much untapped potential he had. Sometimes I wondered if he'd stared too long at the microwave when it was cooking popcorn like Mom told us not to. She said that it could interrupt our brain waves.

Whatever the reason, I figured that when Randy

read the letter, he'd be so overwhelmed with excitement, raging hormones, and all that stuff that he wouldn't think twice.

"Harry?"

I pulled myself out of my daydream to see my math teacher, Mrs. Post, staring at me. Actually, the entire class was staring at me.

"Would you like to share with the class what is so funny?" she asked.

Nixon was two rows up, shaking his head. He told me later that I'd accidentally laughed out loud in the middle of class.

"Nothing, sorry," I answered.

I'd been so anxious to carry out my plan that I wasn't even paying attention.

I tried to keep my thoughts more focused after that. I was pretty sure that even Mrs. Post would be impressed with my plan if I told her about it, but you never know. Grown-ups don't always have the greatest sense of humor, even with really funny stuff.

One time I tried to be funny with my dad when he was working with his tools in the garage. I made up a story that Randy had crashed his bike into a mailbox in the neighborhood next to ours, and that the person whose mailbox he'd flattened was calling the ambulance and also the cops.

The only question was whether Randy would be taken to the hospital or to jail. I'd suggested they pick jail since Randy was a menace to society, but one that had a hospital section within it just to be safe. Then they could keep him locked up for a very long time, since that was probably the safest thing for the whole community.

I figured with news like that, Dad might want to throw a party or say he'd decided to increase my inheritance. At the very least, he might give me a big hug or maybe even a high five, but he didn't think it was funny at all. Dad must have known I was joking, but he still didn't laugh. He just said that making up tall tales was going to get me in trouble someday. Can you believe that?

I told him there wouldn't be much time for me to get myself into trouble since I was constantly on the run from Randy. Dad asked if I'd like to be in trouble right now. I said no, and then I left the garage.

See what I mean? Grown-ups have no sense of humor.

CHAPTER THIRTEEN

By the end of the day, I was ready to burst, but I tried to act normal as I boarded the bus—one of the few places that Randy left me alone. Talking to his friends and trying to flirt with Marcy and the other girls kept him distracted. Giving any attention to a fourth grader like me was beneath him in front of everyone else.

Of course, at home, all bets were off.

Sometimes I wondered if I could get Marcy to live at our house so that he'd be distracted all the time, but I'm not sure my parents would go for that. Actually, I'm not sure Marcy would go for that. It might just be easier if I asked to permanently live at Nixon's house. That would probably solve most of my problems, although I'd miss my mom and dad.

I huddled with Nixon as the middle schoolers

started marching toward the back seats. Marcy came on and sat down with Karen Waits. Randy was close behind, bouncing up the steps with a couple of his buddies. He was laughing and grinning like it was the best day of his life.

I almost felt sorry for him. Almost.

He didn't look my way, which was probably good. That way he wouldn't see my guilty smile.

Nixon and I reviewed the plan's final steps as the bus squealed to a halt at our corner. Nearly half the kids stood up and exited the bus. As the driver pulled away, everyone stood around as usual, talking or throwing a ball for just a few more minutes before splintering off to their houses.

As Randy walked past Marcy, he gave her a big expectant smile. "See you in a few."

She just stared at him with a blank face. Her girl-friends giggled, turned and whispered to each other, and then giggled some more. Everyone was pretty used to seeing Randy act stupid around Marcy, but this was a whole new level.

Every few steps, he'd turn and look at Marcy standing with her friends. The first time, he gave a little wave, which sent the girls into another giggle fest. Then he pointed to his watch, as if to signal that it was almost time.

He looked like such a goof. It was great.

I wondered if it ever occurred to Randy that the letter was too good to be true. That something seemed out of place in the whole situation, kind of like my duck in a bowling alley. As far as I knew, Marcy had never said or done anything remotely like that before, but Randy must have thought it was just a matter of time.

That's the thing with brothers like Randy—they're oblivious to their real problems because they think they're the most important person in the world. Well, pretty soon Randy would have plenty of problems to deal with if my plan worked.

I handed the second walkie-talkie to Nixon with a silent nod and hustled off. I needed to beat Randy home, which shouldn't be hard since he was walking so slowly. But I didn't want to chance it.

There was too much at stake.

CHAPTER FOURTEEN

I ran into the house to set the final pieces of my plan in place. I turned on the video camera by the basement steps, then dialed the volume on the walkie-talkie by the washing machine all the way up.

By the time Randy burst into the house, I was sitting in the kitchen, trying to look casual. He was humming a love song from the radio like a hopeless puppy dog.

"You seem happy," I said, as he walked into the room.

"It's a beautiful day to be a man, Frog Legs," Randy answered. He walked past and tousled my hair.

Normally I'd yell at him for touching me or complain to Mom, but Mom was at the garden center buying fertilizer for her rosebushes, which was part of the reason I'd picked today to execute my plan. Plus, I wanted Randy to stay as happy as possible so he wouldn't expect what was coming next.

The clock on the microwave read 3:42. Three more minutes until the "go time" that I'd arranged with Nixon.

I watched Randy walk into the bathroom and heard him brushing his teeth. He even used mouthwash. Good grief, he must be expecting to kiss her.

Disgusting.

The sound of static squawked from the basement. That was the signal that Nixon was ready. I hoped he could pull everything off on his end. I didn't know what would happen if his parents told him he had to take out the trash or suddenly whisked him off to a piano lesson. That would be a disaster.

This was the riskiest part of the whole plan, but I sensed that it was going to work.

I took a deep breath and walked to the hallway. "Did you hear that noise, Randy?"

His head shot out of the bathroom doorway, eyes open wide. "What noise? Is somebody here?"

He wiped his mouth on a towel. His hair was styled with some gel in a way I'd never seen him wear it before. He looked like he was getting dressed for Halloween but had forgotten to put on the rest of his costume.

Now I just have to say, it was really hard to keep a straight face. I wish I could have frozen that exact moment when he stuck his head out of the bathroom. I knew I had him right where I wanted him, and he had no idea that everything was about to crash down around him.

"It sounded like someone calling your name," I told him. "Didn't you hear it?"

"Okay, take a hike, Frog," Randy said, strutting to the front door.

He paused at the mirror, brushing his fingers through his hair. He frowned and wiped the extra gel on the back of his pants. Gross!

CHAPTER FIFTEEN

I nearly burst out laughing, but I forced myself to stay serious. I couldn't give it away now.

"It sounded like it came from the basement," I said.

"The basement?" Randy asked.

He poked his head out the front door, looking around the empty porch. When he walked back over to me, a voice rang out.

"Randy!"

It was definitely Marcy's voice, and it was definitely coming from the basement.

Randy's head perked up, and he smiled.

"Marcy?" he said, heading toward the basement door.

I think he would have walked straight off a cliff into the Grand Canyon right then. He was totally blind to anything around him except that Marcy was calling his name. I have no idea why Marcy would have been in our basement, of all places, but it didn't matter—Randy wasn't thinking clearly.

"I want to see Randy!" the voice rang out again.

Randy's face looked so excited that I almost fell off my chair. It was working! Little did he know, Nixon was talking to his sister about Randy's odd behavior, asking her questions that would prompt her to say Randy's name. Nixon was then holding down the talk button on the second walkie-talkie at just the right times.

Mom always says that we only hear what we want to hear. I don't know what she'd say about this situation, but Randy was definitely blinded by love and wasn't paying attention to reality.

"Marcy?" Randy called down the steps, opening the basement door.

"Randy, kiss me!" Marcy's voice shouted out from below.

That was more than enough. Randy bolted down the stairs.

Nixon was doing awesome!

He told me later that he'd actually asked Marcy if she wanted Randy to kiss her, and she had responded, "I would never want to have *Randy kiss me!*" Nixon had held down the button for just the last three words.

It was pure genius, if I did say so myself.

When Randy reached the bottom step, I sprang to action, slamming the basement door shut, pushing the lock, and hitting the light switch.

Now we'd see how *Randy* liked the dark.

The pitch-black dark.

CHAPTER SIXTEEN

I cranked up the thermostat to kick on the heat and get the furnace monster growling. Then, right on cue, Nixon turned on spooky Halloween music and played it through the walkie-talkie.

Randy hadn't played any scary music for me, but I figured I could step it up a notch. He had it coming.

I sat back down at the table and waited, picturing big bad Randy down there in the pitch-black dark, imagining the furnace growling with its glowing red eyes, and hearing Nixon's scary music blaring.

It was perfect.

I thought about the frog in the pot, but this time the frog had Randy's face. It was croaking and ribbitting as I stood over the stove with a sinister grin, stirring the water with a long wooden spoon like a sorcerer.

It was like I was finally getting even for all the wrongs he'd committed on me.

I finally had him exactly where I wanted him.

What I didn't picture was what happened next.

I'd figured that Randy would start banging on the door, yelling murderous threats at me, and sure enough, after a moment of quiet, I heard his footsteps tearing up the steps. He started banging on the door like a crazy man. But instead of cursing and yelling threats as I'd expected, he was screaming and whimpering.

He actually sounded really scared.

"Harry!" he wailed. "Let me out of here, Harry!"

Wait a minute.

Was he serious?

He was probably just trying to trick me. If I let my guard down and opened the door now, he'd just tackle me and pummel me. I'd been fooled before.

But he sounded serious...

"Let me out of here, Harry! Help! I can't be down here in the dark!" His words broke between sobs. Was he crying?

This was too weird.

I remembered the video camera, recording Randy's every word. This was exactly what I'd wanted, but now that it was happening, I felt a little sorry for him.

A thought in the back of my mind wondered if

getting revenge wasn't as fun as I'd imagined it to be. Maybe sinking down to Randy's level was going to do me more harm than good.

I paused and leaned against the wall by the door. "What's the matter, Randy? Did Marcy break up with you again?"

I wasn't quite ready to let him off the hook.

"Harry, open the door! I'm sorry for locking you down here before. I won't do it again, just let me out!"

"What's wrong, big brother? Don't you like it in the pitch-black dark?"

"NO!" he screamed. "I'm afraid of the dark, okay? I'm afraid of the dark. I admit it! You have to let me out of here!"

Whoa.

CHAPTER SEVENTEEN

I sat down on the floor in the hallway. What was happening? *Randy* was afraid of the dark? How could that be?

Why had he locked *me* down there if he was scared too? It either explained a lot or made things even more confusing, I wasn't sure which.

"Harry? Are you there?" Randy's voice called again. "Come on, let me out of here. I'm not kidding!"

I decided he was telling the truth, so I stood up and leaned my head to the door. Even if I was going to be nice, there wasn't any reason I couldn't use this opportunity to make things better for me down the road.

"Promise me that you won't ever lock me down there again."

"I promise!" Randy answered.

"Say the whole thing!"

"Harry! I promise I will never lock you down in the basement again. Now turn the light on, will you!"

"And admit that you're in love with Marcy Hawkins," I added, just for fun.

Hey, who knows when I'd have Randy in that position again. I'd better make the most of it while the camera was rolling.

"What? Just let me out of here, Harry!" Randy begged.

"After you say it."

"I love Marcy, okay? I love Marcy! Now let me out of here!"

That should do it.

I flipped the light on and opened the door. Randy fell through the doorway and crumpled onto the floor. His face was bright red and his eyes looked swollen from crying. He didn't look at me, he just slowly picked himself up and marched, defeated, toward his room.

"Remember, you promised!" I called after him.

Randy didn't answer, but I was pretty sure he would stick to his word. Just in case, I took the video camera down from the shelf.

Hey, it's never a bad thing to have an insurance policy.

Every once in a while, Nixon and I watch the video for a good laugh, but I don't think I'll need to use it. I thought about using the tape to blackmail Randy into dressing up like a duck and going to the bowling alley in front of Marcy, but that would have been too much.

Mom is always telling us two wrongs don't make a right and that sort of thing. While that's probably true, having an older brother like Randy can make things like that confusing for a kid.

Things with Randy weren't perfect after that, but they did get better for a few months. He may have just been scared I'd trick him into going back into the dark basement now that I knew his secret fear, but I prefer to think that I gained a little of his respect by managing to fool him so badly. Either way, it was nice not to be bullied so much.

Soon we even convinced our dad to get an electrician to install a second light and a switch at the bottom of the basement stairs so it wasn't so dark.

After all, nobody likes to be locked in the dark.

Especially the pitch-black dark.

CHAPTER EIGHTEEN

Once school let out, however, things started to go downhill fast. Maybe Randy and I could only hold a truce for so long, or maybe summer vacation was just giving everyone too much free time.

Sometimes I think it's good for us to be in school, since it keeps Randy occupied with classes, homework, and football practice. The more he's thinking about other stuff, the less time he has to torment me. Mom says that we all need structure in our lives to keep us occupied so we don't get into trouble.

I suppose that goes for me too. Normally the trouble in my life starts with a capital R and ends in y, but I made a few bad decisions too this summer, if you can believe it. But even when something is my fault, Randy finds a way to make it complicated.

Like when I tried to mow the lawn.

That might not sound like a very big mistake. Mowing the lawn probably sounds like a helpful thing to do. It might even qualify someone for an extra big allowance.

Well, maybe for some kids, and perhaps even someday for me too, but right now, as a ten-year-old, I'm probably not ready yet to use our lawn mower. You'll probably agree with me when you hear what happened.

We have a big backyard, so my dad uses a riding tractor—you know the kind I mean, it's bright green and yellow with big tires. My dad says that if he had to do our whole backyard with one of those little push mowers it would take forever, and he doesn't have forever. He says he barely has today, with all the traveling he does for his job.

He's gone most of the time, which kind of stinks, since it's fun to have your dad around to do stuff with like throw a football or go on a campout. It would also be one more person to keep an eye on Randy.

Mom keeps trying to get Dad to hire one of those lawn services that descend on your house like a giant swarm of bees and finish everything in no time, but Dad says that costs too much. He says God gave him two sons for a reason, and that someday we'll be doing all the yard work instead of him.

Randy grumbled about that for like a week, saying he didn't care about doing chores, but Dad trained him on how to use the mower anyway. They had a really long talk about being responsible and making wise decisions and about how such a big machine is not a toy to fool around with.

I happened to be passing by during parts of Dad's speech. It was one of those that just keeps going on and on and on.

For a minute I thought he was teaching Randy how to *build* a lawn mower, but he was just repeating everything like fifty times to make sure Randy got it. I caught the first part on the way to get the mail, and I heard the end of it on my way out to Nixon's house twenty minutes later.

I couldn't help but wonder if Dad remembered that it was Randy he was talking to. Responsibility and making wise choices aren't terms normally used to describe my big brother. But for some reason, Dad seemed convinced that it would be okay, and I have to admit, Randy did seem to do a good job.

CHAPTER NINETEEN

At the beginning of summer, I told my dad that *I* actually *wanted* to help out, and that I'd be happy to drive the riding mower.

He said I wasn't old enough yet to operate it unsupervised, but he agreed to give me a mini-lesson about how the mower worked—how to start it, brake, go forward, and turn the mower blades on. There was a lot to remember about which button or lever did what, but I figured if Randy was smart enough to do it, I could handle it no problem.

A couple days later, Nixon was over at my house, and I couldn't help but open my big mouth and brag about knowing how to mow.

"I've never seen you on that tractor," Nixon said.

"Honest, my dad showed me how," I answered.

Mom always tells us we shouldn't try to make

ourselves look important by bragging or exaggerating, but in this case, it was really true. I *had* driven the tractor in the yard. Of course, I conveniently left out the fact that my dad was standing right next to me and I'd only driven it for a couple minutes, but I *did* drive it.

Well, Nixon didn't believe me, so I figured there wouldn't be much harm in giving him a little demo of my sweet new skills. Mom had run to the store and Dad was at work, so I had no choice but to start the big machine up on my own. I even put Dad's noise-canceling headphones on so I would look professional.

Nixon seemed impressed, although I couldn't tell what he actually said through the headphones.

Everything was going fine as I pulled the mower out of the shed. I went down the side of the yard and then turned back for a second pass. I even went in kind-of-straight lines, which was how I'd seen all the professional landscapers do it. Someday I wanted to try to make fancy patterns like they did on the field at professional baseball stadiums, but I wasn't ready for that yet.

I figured I'd done enough and was about to put the mower away, when things started to go off the rails, as my dad would say.

I tried to turn down the motor to ask Nixon what

he thought of my excellent driving, but I must have hit the wrong lever because I suddenly started moving in reverse. I hadn't expected that, and before I knew it, I was moving faster and faster across the lawn. I tried to stop, but in the excitement, I completely forgot what all the controls did.

Nixon started jumping and waving his arms like he was a third-base coach trying to tell me to slide underneath the tag at home plate. He was yelling something, but I couldn't understand it because I was still wearing the headphones.

I ripped them off just in time to hear him yell, "Look out! Behind you!"

I looked behind me and my breath caught.

I was heading directly toward Mom's rose garden.

CHAPTER TWENTY

W ell, as you can imagine, I was pretty panicked at this point.

I frantically pushed what I thought was the brake, but I must have pressed the wrong pedal, because the tractor only went faster.

In no time, I was right on top of the roses. The back tire of the mower banged into the edge of the stone patio, stopping my progress but keeping me positioned directly over the rosebushes.

The mower blades ripped through branch after branch of the precious plants. Shredded petals and leaves shot out the side of the mower and up into the air like confetti on New Year's Eve. I can still hear the chomping sound in my head.

It was awful.

Everything was a bit of a blur until I eventually

found the right lever to move the engine out of reverse and then drove forward into the middle of the yard.

There was an eerie silence when the engine finally died. Nixon was just standing on the patio, his eyes as wide as dinner plates, watching what I'd done.

I jumped off the mower and ran back to the rose garden, staring in horror at the giant hacking cuts to the middle bush. Petals and leaves were strewn all around, like some kind of giant beast had attacked the plants and then moved on.

My mom loves roses.

Actually, that might be an understatement. Tending to her rose garden is her favorite thing in the whole world.

Well, maybe after her family, or at least, after me and Dad. I'm not sure where Randy fits on her list, but he'd definitely be a little further down on mine.

She spends time nearly every day tending to the roses: pruning them, watering them, weeding the beds —honestly, I don't even know what else she does out there with them.

Randy told me that sometimes he's even heard her talking to them. If you ask me, that's just weird, but I haven't told my mom that. I guess if it makes her happy, then why not. If I had Randy as a son, I'd probably start talking to the plants too.

So when I saw what I'd done to her roses, her favorite, beloved roses, I thought I might puke. (I didn't, but that would have been the icing on the cake, puking all over the mangled roses, don't you think?)

I tried to catch my breath and looked around to make sure no one else besides Nixon had witnessed my disaster.

That's when I saw him.

You can probably guess who. That's right, it was Randy, standing casually beside the house, watching the whole scene unfold. He'd probably been there from the start, but of course he didn't try to help. A creepy smile stretched across his lips as he stood there, shaking his head slowly.

"Help me," I cried, now trying to figure out how to get the mower back in the shed before Mom got home.

Randy sauntered over to us, chuckling softly. "This is going to cost you, Frog Legs," he said, but then he started the mower up and drove it smoothly back into the shed. Then, amazingly, he walked out with a rake and tidied up the strewn branches and petals.

"What good is that going to do?" asked Nixon, still standing by nervously.

He looked like there were a hundred other places he'd rather be, but he couldn't remember how to move. Kind of like when you drive by a car accident on the highway and can't help but stare. You feel bad for the people involved, but you're also kind of grateful that it wasn't you. That was the kind of look on Nixon's face right then.

"Making it not look quite so obvious," Randy answered coolly, with the confidence of someone who'd done his fair share of cleaning up after disasters. "I'm covering up the *frog prints*. Ha, ha." He nudged Nixon and laughed at his own joke.

I wasn't quite sure what he thought could explain how the bushes looked now, his frog prints joke aside. Maybe they would look like they'd been attacked by a velociraptor or, more likely, some kind of mutant, radioactive deer.

Do deer even like rosebushes?

"Thanks," I managed to say, just as Nixon announced he was going home. He'd wisely decided he didn't want to be anywhere near whatever my parents (or more likely, Randy) were going to do to me.

Anytime Randy acted the least amount helpful or friendly toward us, we started trying to guess what bad things he had in mind down the road.

Whatever came from this was sure to be a doozy.

CHAPTER TWENTY-ONE

I t wasn't easy getting to sleep that night. Normally the things keeping me up would be my dark closet or Randy's bad intentions, but this time all I could think about were Mom's roses.

It had been nearly dark by the time she got home, and she'd never ventured close enough to the backyard to see the disaster. Even so, each time she drew closer to the back window over the course of the evening, I felt like I might puke.

Thankfully, she did most of her gardening in the mornings. That gave me more time to think of an explanation, but I feared it was only putting off the inevitable.

She was going to kill me.

I guess I finally drifted off to sleep that night,

because when I woke up, it was morning. Actually, something woke me up.

Mom screaming.

I held my breath and closed my eyes. Maybe I was still asleep. Maybe this entire situation was just a bad dream and I'd never shown the lawn mower to Nixon in the first place. Mom's roses could still be perfect.

I opened my eyes, but it was still morning, and I still heard the screaming. For a moment, I wondered if Mom was in trouble and was screaming for help. That was, until I heard the words she was saying. Some of them I can't really repeat, but I did hear the word *roses* in there.

I was so dead meat.

It was no use delaying my death, so I slid out of bed and tiptoed to the window. I looked down into the backyard, right over top of Mom's garden, but then I did a double take at what I saw.

Three big dogs were tearing around our backyard. Mom was chasing them with a rake, but they kept dodging her like they were playing a game of tag.

What was happening?

I recognized one of the dogs as Mr. Bruner's Great Dane from down the street but wasn't sure who the other two were. I hurried outside to the patio where Randy was trying to calm Mom down.

"Shoo! Get out of here, you mangy beasts!" she yelled.

"What's going on?" I asked Randy.

He looked down at me with a mischievous grin.

"Dogs."

"Yes, I can see that there are dogs, Randy, but what are they doing here? Why are they in our backyard, and why is Mom yelling at them?"

Randy grinned again and pointed over at the flower garden. "Look what they did to Mom's rosebushes."

I hesitated for a second, but then looked at the scene of yesterday's butchery. They say a killer always revisits the scene of the crime, and that morning it felt like a giant sign was on my forehead that read "guilty."

I looked closer at the rosebushes, but something wasn't right. They weren't as we'd left them the day before. Randy had raked the petals and smoothed out the tire tracks, but all around the bushes were piles of dirt and holes where something had been digging —like dogs.

I turned back to Randy with a dumfounded look just as Mom stormed over to us.

"Can you believe it?" she huffed. "Just look at what those dogs have done to my rosebushes!"

I shook my head. I couldn't believe it.

All the evidence of my lawn mower massacre was

completely erased by the mess from the dogs. It was terrible, yet a miracle at the same time. A yellow dog made a quick dash back toward the holes, but Mom headed him off again with the rake.

I looked at Randy. "That's incredible."

"Yep," he answered. "It's almost like somebody planned it." He put his hand on his chin. "Somebody really smart."

My eyes opened wider as I tried to think of what could have happened.

"But I'll tell you, Frog Legs," Randy continued. "Whoever was smart enough to pull all this together is probably going to be owed big time by whoever benefited from it. You follow what I'm saying?"

He bent down and winked at me. "Big time."

CHAPTER TWENTY-TWO

Amazingly, Mom was convinced that the dogs were responsible for ruining her rosebushes. She never even asked me if I had run over them with the lawn mower. I guess that was natural, given that she caught three big dogs digging them up, but I was still relieved.

A few days later, Randy fessed up (to me at least) and admitted that he'd buried a few chunks of meat in the ground under the rosebushes and then coaxed the neighbors' dogs into our backyard. He said he'd seen a cover-up like that on a TV show one time.

I didn't tell him this, but I had to admit, it was genius.

It was very unlike Randy.

It made me wonder if I'd underestimated him. Maybe he had a lot of untapped potential, just like me.

But mostly, I was worried, because the only reason Randy would do something nice like that for me was so he could hold it as leverage for me to do something he wanted.

I really felt bad for Mom, but I reasoned that the roses were already messed up now, and at least she was mad at some dogs rather than her own son. Something like that can really cause a lot of stress in a mother-child relationship.

At least that's what Nixon told me one time on the bus. He said he'd seen that on a TV show his sister was watching. Maybe I need to start paying more attention to the shows I always figured were boring. There seems to be a lot of handy stuff in them.

I don't know if all of that is true, but I am glad Mom didn't know it was me. Maybe someday when I'm older, like twenty, when she won't be mad about it anymore, I'll tell her it was really me.

I nearly broke down and told her anyway one morning when she proposed that Randy and I hang out together for the day. Dad was away on another business trip, and she had to go downtown for a business meeting over lunch.

"Boys, I want the two of you to get along today," she said. "There's no reason you can't spend time together and keep out of trouble."

"Mom, I really don't think that's a good idea," I said, glancing out of the corner of my eye to see if Randy was listening.

Getting along around the house was one thing, but the prospect of us hanging out together for an afternoon in public with no one else around for him to focus his attention on gave me the chills.

"Oh come on, Harry," Randy said, walking over and putting his arm around me. "We'll have fun." He flashed a totally fake smile, but Mom seemed to buy it. "You can count on us, Mom."

You'd think that after thirteen years of having Randy for a son, my mom would be better at spotting his fake smile, but she believes him more often than I'd expect. I've tried to tell her that Randy can't be trusted, that even when he says he'll be nice, he almost always isn't.

I think she's one of those people who likes to think the best of people rather than the worst. I agree with her, most of the time, but when you run across someone like Randy, all bets are off. Maybe she was distracted this time because of the meeting she had to attend. Grown-ups seem to get that way sometimes when they have something important to do.

"Perfect," said Mom. "There's a movie playing at

two o'clock, and you can get lunch right across the street from my office before that."

"Um, I don't know..." I started.

"That sounds fun," said Randy, nudging me in the side. "Right, Harry?"

"Uh, huh," I answered, not too enthusiastically.

As soon as Mom walked out of the room, Randy bounced his eyebrows menacingly. He silently mouthed the word, "Rosebushes."

I gulped, trying not to think of all the things that could go wrong.

CHAPTER TWENTY-THREE

"Come on, Frog Legs, get over here!"

I cringed at the sound of Randy's voice coming from the bushes. We were supposed to be at the movies. At least that's what I wanted to do.

That's what Mom thought we were doing too, but right when we were headed toward the theater, Randy grabbed my arm and pulled me across the street toward the park that runs along the river next to downtown. We'd eaten lunch at the sandwich place across from Mom's office before Randy decided on the detour.

At first the park wasn't so bad. We looked out at the water and tried to see who could get the most skips with flat rocks across the surface. I had a really good one that had twelve skips. Randy didn't like that, so he tried to skip one off of my leg, which kind of hurt, but I tried not to show it. I was just grateful he didn't try to skip it off my head. That's the kind of thing that could give a person a concussion, you know.

We walked out onto a little bridge that extends partially into the river, throwing more stones and trying to hit a giant whirlpool a little ways away that seemed to come from a big drain under the water. That was when Randy started talking to a girl he saw from school, so I just stood and stared at the white water.

It churned up and under and around like suds in a washing machine. It was mesmerizing, and I stared for a long time, glad to be up on the bridge and not down in the water. I'd probably be chopped to bits or sucked down into the drain and shot out somewhere in the middle of the ocean if I got caught in that.

After Randy finally stopped jabbering with the girl, we started wandering through a secluded part of the wooded trail further up the river. The air-conditioned darkness of the theater sure seemed better right now than this hot, humid day with Randy. I even thought I saw a mosquito the size of a popsicle.

The park was nice, but I didn't like wandering through the woods by ourselves when no one knew where we were. Not that I thought anything terrible would happen. It wasn't like there was going to be a masked killer with a chainsaw or something down there, but being alone with Randy was bad enough.

I followed a narrow trail through the thick under-growth toward Randy's voice. I didn't see him until I reached the water's edge.

"What are you doing?" I asked suspiciously.

"Check it out!" Randy grinned, perching his foot on the side of an old canoe. He acted like we were going to be Lewis and Clark or some other great explorers.

I stared warily across the river, leaning out to see just a glimpse of white water downstream. I had a sinking feeling in my stomach.

"Whose canoe is that?" I asked, already knowing what he'd say.

"It's ours, now."

"Right..." I looked back toward the main trail. "I don't think so, Randy."

Grand theft canoe.

That had to be a felony.

CHAPTER TWENTY-FOUR

I stared down at the old canoe and shook my head. It looked like I could kick a hole right through its thin wooden boards.

"I'm not getting in that thing. It'll probably sink."

"Come on," said Randy. "We're going."

"Where?"

"Just a little ways down the river. We'll get out up near the bridge where we started. It'll be fine. Why shouldn't we explore a little?"

I stood where I was, not moving my feet from the dry ground. I tried to think of where to start with my objections.

"First of all, Mom thinks we're at the movies. Second, that is not our canoe, and I highly doubt that it is just sitting there for people to borrow. Third—"

A shower of small pebbles rained down on my

head. "Ow!" I reached my hands up for protection. "Cut it out."

"Okay, have it your way, Frog." Randy lifted an end of the canoe and dragged it into the edge of the river. "I'll just have a little talk with Mom when we get back about what really happened to her roses."

"Sure, tell her, I don't care," I answered, trying to sound confident, but feeling my heart beat a little faster as Randy stood there on the bank of the river, a paddle in his hand.

As much as it had worked out well in some ways by blaming the neighbors' unruly dogs, I knew someday Randy would use it against me and I almost wished Mom already knew. It just wasn't in his nature to do something only to be helpful. There had to be a catch.

Well, it looked like today was payback.

I stared downstream at the white water and gulped. It was either risk my life with Randy or face Mom's wrath about the roses, and I didn't like either of my options.

I thought for a moment of reminding Randy of the videotape from the basement, but right then I didn't know if it would even matter. He had one of those looks in his eyes that said he was going to do what he wanted, regardless of what I said.

If there was any hope left in my mind about

whether the goodwill we'd built up during the end of the school year would last, it was clear now that it was officially over.

"Don't be scared." Randy lifted a lone faded orange life vest from inside the canoe. "This one's specially sized for frogs like you."

He placed two wooden paddles inside the canoe and shot me an angry look. "Now *get in*."

CHAPTER TWENTY-FIVE

I eyed the woods around us, making sure no one was watching, then climbed into the front of the canoe, trying to keep my sneakers from getting wet.

"Are you sure you know what you're doing?" I looked back at Randy as he pushed off from the shore and jumped into the back of the canoe.

"Relax, Frog Legs. I've got this." He lifted his paddle and dipped it into the water, pushing against the shallow riverbed to keep us moving forward.

I hate that word. *Relax*. And the name *Frog Legs* too, but I guess I'm getting used to that. Every time my brother told me to relax, I knew there was going to be trouble. He was only three years older than me, but I'd learned that his view of what was fun was very different than mine.

Mom says older brothers are like that. I think it stinks.

I picked up the second paddle and tried to copy Randy's strokes. "So whose canoe is this again?"

"I told you, it's the park's."

"And they won't mind that we're taking it?"

"We're not taking it, we're just borrowing it." Randy shook his head as he dug his paddle into the water. "It's here for people to use."

I still wasn't so sure about that, but it was too late to argue with him since we were already drifting down the river to our doom. I shouldn't have gotten in this stupid old canoe in the first place. I looked down at the lines of wear in the wood. It was a miracle it was even floating.

"Just shut up and paddle," Randy said, as if reading my mind. The canoe bounced over something with an eerie scraping sound. "And keep a lookout for rocks."

"Was that a rock?" I stared down into the water, but it was too dark to see to the bottom.

"Yep."

How was I going to call out rocks when I couldn't even see them?

"What happens if there's a rock?" I asked.

Randy grinned. "We turn. Or we hit it. But turning would be better."

My eyes opened wide. "What happens if we hit it?"

"You have that thing for a reason," Randy answered, pointing down at my feet to the ratty-looking life jacket. It didn't look like it could hold itself up in the water, let alone me, but I picked it up and strapped it on nonetheless. Something was better than nothing.

I gulped as we moved along in the water.

This was not good.

CHAPTER TWENTY-SIX

W e drifted further downriver, the current moving us along without much effort on our parts. I lifted my paddle out of the water since it didn't feel like I was really doing much anyway.

I looked back at Randy. He was holding his paddle behind him in the water like a rudder. It actually looked like he knew what he was doing. Whether it was because of him or just luck, we seemed to be staying in the right direction.

I took a deep breath and tried to relax. This wasn't half-bad. The sun was out, the breeze was blowing against my face, and we hadn't sunk.

I slowly started to get a little more comfortable. Randy hadn't done anything crazy yet, and it was pretty smooth gliding along the river in the canoe, especially with Randy doing all the work in the back. Maybe this was one of those things that he was really good at, like mowing the lawn. It was possible that he had more secret talents I didn't know about.

"This is kind of fun," I caught myself saying before I knew it. I hadn't actually meant to say that out loud.

"I told you it would be great," Randy scoffed. "Why are you always doubting me?" He smirked at me like any concerns I'd had for my safety had been utterly ridiculous. As if every day with Randy was smooth sailing.

I shook my head. It was unbelievable how he could twist the facts all around when he wanted things to go his way. I tried to remind myself not to be too comfortable. Randy had a way of lulling me into a false sense of security just before the hammer dropped. There are expressions like "the calm before the storm" for a reason. That one was probably first said by a kid with an older brother a lot like Randy.

If I had a dollar, heck, even a quarter, for every time Randy acted like something was going to be fun but it turned out terrible, I'd be rolling in dough. I could even buy a brand-new canoe at the really big sporting goods store with the escalator and then have a professional instructor teach me how to paddle and all the proper safety techniques. Then I'd get my awesome canoe next to Randy's in the river and challenge him to a race.

Of course, I'd smoke him, and then I'd walk away with a giant trophy. Mom and Dad would be there cheering for me. Nixon could even be my first mate and help me navigate. Oh, and Marcy could be there to laugh at Randy too, that would be the icing on the cake. It would be epic.

Sure, that wouldn't be a very *nice* thing to do. Come to think of it, it was probably the exact kind of thing Mom was always talking to me about. (No, not the untapped potential thing, that was Ms. Stitch.) I mean, treating others the way I wanted to be treated. That was another one of her favorite things to say. I don't know, I suppose she's right, but that is just so hard to do when you have an older brother like Randy.

I told Mom once that if *I* was the older brother and Randy was the younger brother, I would treat him much better. She said it was hard to know exactly what someone would do until you've been in the other person's shoes. I told her maybe she and Dad should have another kid, and then I could be the older brother and we could try it out.

She said I should just go do my homework.

CHAPTER TWENTY-SEVEN

The water was growing choppier as we moved further into the river. I glanced back at the shore longingly. The river was quickly becoming the kind of place you don't want to be with just an inexperienced thirteen-year-old and a rickety, old wooden canoe.

I'd never even been in a canoe. Randy claimed to have been in one when he went camping with his friend Lance Peterson one time last year, but I doubted it. He'd also said he had caught a largemouth bass that was two feet long. He tends to exaggerate.

I looked up on the shore and saw the trail that we'd followed before our foolish venture into the water. It seemed much safer up on dry land. A crazy masked killer with a chainsaw in the woods might have been better than floating to my death on the river with

Randy. I started to second-guess whether the truth about Mom's rosebushes was worth this.

I focused back on the water ahead as we rounded a bend. Swirls of white-colored water came into view like dozens of tiny hot tubs. As the swirls grew closer, it dawned on me what they were—rapids!

"Turn!" I yelled. "I see rocks! Rapids ahead!"

I twisted back and saw Randy laugh, his face in a devilish smile. "Hold on, Frog Legs."

"What?" I cried back at him, cinching the bottom strap on my life jacket tighter until I could hardly breathe. I pulled on the upper strap, but it broke off in my hand. I held it up to show Randy, when all of a sudden our canoe hit the edge of the white water and jerked forward like we were on the log flume ride at the water park. I had to grab ahold of the side of the canoe just to keep my balance.

"Randyyyy!!" I screamed, as we flew over a sharp, slippery descent toward our doom.

Our canoe dipped and dived along the rapids. I didn't call out the rocks. I just squeezed the side of the canoe with all my might and tried to keep my eyes open.

That's when I saw it. Dead ahead.

There was a huge rock, standing out of the water like an iceberg about to hit the Titanic.

"Rock!" I screamed at the top of my lungs. I turned to see if Randy heard me.

This time, his eyes were wide too, the smile wiped from his face. He mumbled something under his breath that didn't sound like a very nice word.

"Paddle left!" he ordered. "Hard!"

I reached down and grabbed my paddle, fumbling to get it in the water. I saw the huge rock getting closer from the corner of my eye as I stuck my paddle into the water, but the force of the current was so strong it ripped the paddle right from my hands.

"No!" I yelled, reaching out with my other hand to grab it.

As I stretched for the paddle, the canoe tilted to the side, just as we went over another big dip. The top edge of the canoe dropped to the waterline, dragging over a submerged rock with a terrible sound.

I watched as a hole tore across the side of the canoe, as if a T-Rex had ripped it open with a giant claw. Buckets of water began to pour in, and before I could even call out to Randy, I lost my balance and tumbled out into the river.

CHAPTER TWENTY-EIGHT

This was it—the end for me—I could feel it.

It was worse than anything I'd encountered before, worse than any practical joke Randy had ever played. Worse than the pitch-black dark, the fire-breathing furnace in the basement, or even Mom's yet to be experienced wrath about the rosebushes. I was going to drown out here, alone on the river with Randy with no one to save me, while Mom thought I was at the movies.

I was sinking, floating, flailing through the cold water. I couldn't see Randy or the canoe through the water in my eyes. My screams were sucked up by the sounds of the rushing water all around me. My crusty old life jacket seemed to be keeping me on the surface, but I was zipping through the rapids.

For a moment, I thought I might pass out. I started

smelling popcorn from the movie theater, and then I saw flower petals floating all around me in the rapids. The sound of the water whizzing by me kind of sounded like the roar of the lawn mower as it tore through the rosebushes.

I imagined Nixon floating by on a boat in the shape of a lawn mower. He was shaking his head sadly. "You should never have gotten in the canoe," his voice said, but it was deep and slow, like when you play something at half speed.

I tried to snap back to reality, wiping the spray from my eyes. The canoe was farther up ahead, floating at an awkward angle, the front half sunk into the river. Randy was balancing in the back with a wild look on his face, searching for me across the water. He looked scared.

Somehow at that moment, I made a decision. I wasn't going to let that river beat me. I wasn't going to let *Randy* beat me. Not today.

I'm not really sure what made me change my mind. Maybe it was the cold water, or maybe I just got a shot of adrenaline, but I decided I was going to survive, with or without Randy's help.

With my legs stuck out in front of me, I bounced awkwardly off the rocks like I was in a pinball machine, my arms and knees banging against rocks that I couldn't even see.

For a moment, I was stuck in a backflow. I reached out and grabbed on to a rock, providing a few seconds to catch my breath and think. I knew I probably wouldn't drown if I kept my face toward the sky. If I could just make it through the rapids without banging my head on a rock, I might be okay.

I wiped my face with my left hand, but my right slipped off the rock and I was pulled back into the current. I managed to avoid any major crashes with rocks, but I knew I was going to have serious bruises tomorrow. Randy was paddling madly up ahead, trying to make the half-sunk canoe head against the current, but it was no use. He was moving farther and farther away.

Finally, I shot out of the bottom of the rapids and floated into the open water. I could see Randy and the canoe ahead of me. I waved my hands in the air to get his attention until he finally saw me. A wave of relief filled his face. I wondered if he'd been worried about me. Maybe he'd wondered if he'd finally gone too far with his hairbrained ideas.

CHAPTER TWENTY-NINE

As I floated toward Randy's canoe, I saw the bridge where we'd walked and thrown rocks earlier in the day stretched out behind him in the distance. Randy's canoe was almost completely sunk now.

"Harry!" he yelled out to me as I floated closer. "Are you okay?" He stretched his paddle out toward me.

I lunged for it, but my hand slipped off the wet wood. He extended it again, and this time I grabbed higher on the paddle with both hands.

"Got it!" I said, pulling myself toward the canoe.

Randy stood up in the canoe and tried to reel me in. I purposely yanked on the paddle harder than I needed to, sending Randy tumbling into the river next to me with a belly flop.

"Harry!" He kicked his way back over to where I was hanging on to the half-sunk canoe.

I actually laughed, seeing the look on Randy's face. I felt better now that the rapids were behind us. I was also glad not to be alone anymore, even if it meant I was with Randy. It seemed like we were going to make it.

"Relax," I said with a chuckle. It was good to give Randy a taste of his own medicine sometimes.

"Did you hurt yourself on the rocks?" Randy asked.

For a moment I wondered if he really did care about me. I thought about saying something mean back, but instead I just shook my head. "Nah, I don't think so."

"I guess that probably wasn't such a good idea, huh?" Randy said, attempting a weak smile. "They probably should do better inspections on those canoes if they're going to leave them lying around for people to use."

I raised my eyebrows. Surely he had to be kidding. I opened my mouth to say something, when I noticed a flurry of activity on the bridge up ahead. Several people were waving their hands. Were they waving at us? I raised my hand and waved back, balancing myself with my other arm.

"What's their problem?" Randy asked.

"Probably just afraid we can't swim," I answered. I tugged again on the orange life jacket, now bunched up around my neck but still working well to keep me afloat.

"Hello!" I yelled. "We're okay. He's a maniac, but we're alive!"

Randy chuckled, then grabbed the canoe more tightly. Soon we could hear yelling from the people who were now waving their hands even more frantically.

"Are they just happy that we reached each other?" I said. "What's that they're swinging over the side of the bridge? Is that a rope?"

Randy shook his head. "I don't know what the big deal is, we were just—"

He stopped mid-sentence as we both realized at the same time what they were yelling. I think it was because we heard the roar. Not like the sound of the rapids, or even like a lawn mower whacking through rosebushes. This sounded like a waterfall.

Then I remembered the whirlpool.

We were headed straight for it.

CHAPTER THIRTY

"Kick toward the bridge," Randy shouted, remembering the whirlpool at the same time I did.

The canoe sunk down lower in the water as we struggled to keep a hold on it and move at the same time. We were going too fast and were wide of the bridge. We were going to miss the rope.

"We're not going to make it!" I shouted.

Suddenly I was angry again. Angry at Randy for bringing me out on this insane ride of death down the river, and mad at myself for agreeing to come even though I knew better. I was even mad at Mom for making us hang out together in the first place. How many things going wrong did it take for her to realize that Randy was not good for me, that someday he was going to go too far, and this war of ours would end, probably with my death? Well, she'd be sorry *then*, when she didn't have me around anymore. That was for sure.

"Let go of the canoe!" shouted Randy over the growing roar of the water.

"What?" I said, shaking my head. He was crazy. We needed the canoe to float.

"Let go!" repeated Randy. "It's too heavy. We can swim without it."

I hesitated, but Randy stared into my eyes and nodded, his face suddenly looking calm and confident. I wondered if this was one of those false sense of security times again. Trusting Randy was what had gotten me into this mess, but he did seem sure of himself, and I didn't have a better plan.

Even though it was his fault we were in a fight against nature, against the elements, we had to band together. I had to trust him.

I glanced up at the approaching whirlpool, swallowed hard, and released my grip on the canoe. Randy grabbed my life jacket and pushed us away from the canoe with his legs. We drifted and kicked, still gaining speed as we approached the whirlpool. But we were gradually moving closer to the bridge where the water was slowing down.

The canoe stayed in the fast-moving current,

moving farther away from us as it accelerated toward the whirlpool. I watched its bow sink down like it was headed off a cliff, the back end sticking up in the air like the Titanic. Then it disappeared. I imagined it smashing into bits and for once was suddenly glad I'd listened to Randy.

I looked back to the bridge where two men stood against the railing swinging a brightly colored rope over the side, like the kind they used to climb rocks. As we drew closer, I began to feel the tug of the current trying to drag us back toward the whirlpool again.

It was now or never.

Randy and I both stretched our hands up to the sky, reaching for the dangling rope. Randy reached it first, but missed.

"No!" he yelled.

I grabbed at it with my right hand, but the rope pulled right through my fingers. I made one more desperate swipe with my left hand, and this time it held strong. "Grab on!"

Randy clutched my leg as the men pulled on the rope. We were like a human chain, struggling to keep our heads above the water. The crowd on the bridge was shouting. They were cheering for us to make it. Randy was too heavy for them to pull us up to the bridge, so they gradually towed us along the length of the bridge and toward the shore.

Finally, my feet touched the bottom of the riverbed. I hadn't even noticed that my sneakers had fallen off. They had probably been ripped away in the rapids. The river bottom was soft and squishy beneath my socks, but I didn't care.

I let out a deep breath. Randy released his grip on my leg and stood in the water. We both climbed up to the shore and collapsed onto our backs, exhausted, but happy to be alive.

CHAPTER THIRTY-ONE

I shivered, realizing how much worse our little boat trip could have been. Randy was struggling to catch his breath. I should have known better than to follow him into the canoe.

We could have died. Mom definitely wouldn't like that.

Randy turned toward me and attempted a weak smile. "See, I told you there was nothing to worry about."

I raised my eyebrows as the crowd from the bridge made their way down to us.

Randy sat up and extended his hand. "Even?"

I grabbed his hand and pulled myself up. I looked him right in the eye and shook my head. "Not even close."

The people from the bridge let us borrow towels and dry off, but there was no way that we could pretend to Mom that we'd actually been at the movies. Even if our clothes had been dry, I wasn't wearing any shoes now.

Mom wasn't happy when she learned that we'd been in the park instead of the theater like we'd told her we would be. We didn't share all the details about our canoe trip, just that we'd been playing with rocks by the river and fallen in. That wasn't exactly a lie, but it wasn't exactly the whole truth either. Mom said once there's a reason why in a courtroom you have to put your hand on a Bible and swear that you are going to tell the truth, the whole truth and nothing but the truth. It keeps you from leaving out some small details that are important.

I felt as though Randy and I might have formed another little peace treaty thanks to our trip down the river. I'm sure it will end at some point, just like our peace after the basement, but it's nice, no matter how short.

It's also possible that Randy's just starting to mature. It could be those hormones that Mom's always talking about, or maybe Marcy is rubbing off on him. I did feel bad after what I'd done to him in the basement, and also grateful that he covered for me with the rose-bushes (even if he did almost kill me on the river).

So for a while, every time I went over to Nixon's house, I made a point of saying a lot of nice things about Randy around Marcy and her parents. Pretty soon, she was talking to Randy more and they started hanging out. I think she might even like him as much as Tony Morehouse now, but who can really tell with girls.

The thing about older brothers, though, is that just when stuff starts going good, it's bound to take a turn for the worse. It's part of the code, I think, that all big brothers learn when the younger brother comes home from the hospital. Someone must deliver a manual to the house while the parents are all wrapped up in the new baby and not looking. It probably spells out things like how to torment, how to lie and cheat, how to come up with names that are just mean enough to stick. Stuff like that. Sometimes I think maybe Randy *wrote* the manual, he's so good at it. So even though things are good right now, I am not quite ready to believe the worst is behind us.

Mom says that when we're older, Randy and I will probably be friends. I don't know about all that. Right now I'm just concentrating on staying on my toes and keeping watch for Randy and his sinister ways. When you're in a war, you have to stay alert.

Maybe someday the war *will* be over, but in the meantime, it's every brother for himself. And I'm counting on all my untapped potential to give me the upper hand.

ACKNOWLEDGMENTS

I never had a brother. But as the dad of three boys, their antics are pretty natural for me to write about. I've been wanting to start another series in addition to *The Virginia Mysteries*, and Harry and Randy seemed like a nice change of pace to Sam and Derek. They remind me a bit of Kevin and Wayne on *The Wonder Years*, but I think these boys have a bit of every brother relationship in them.

This book started out as two smaller short stories. I'd written *Pitch Black Dark* in 2014 based on a conversation I overheard with my oldest son and his friend. The phrase stuck in my head and things grew from there. I revisited the duo again in a short story called *Rapids Ahead*, part of a middle-grade collection of authors from Richmond, Virginia, titled *River City Secrets*. If you've read either of the short stories previously, I hope you'll still enjoy this book, which is more than twice as long as the original stories.

Thank you as always to my family for providing me the grace to hammer away on my stories at odd and sometimes inconvenient hours, my friends at Richmond Children's Writers for your early critiques of these stories, Lana Krumwiedie and Chop Suey Books for organizing and publishing the short story collection, Kim for your edits, Dane for another awesome cover, the dozens of elementary school librarians, teachers, and students that I've met with over the past several years, and the thousands of readers who have made writing all my stories so enjoyable and truly changed my life.

KEEP READING FOR A PREVIEW OF CABIN ELEVEN

BROTHER WARS BOOK 2

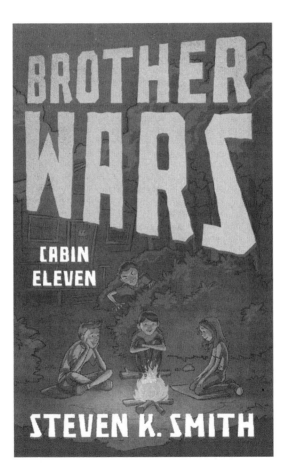

CABIN ELEVEN: CHAPTER ONE

I slid into the seat on the bus next to Nixon. He was leaned over his backpack, searching for something.

"What are you doing?" I asked.

He didn't look up. "I have to show you something."

"Okay," I said, staring out the window. The middle school across the parking lot was letting out. I saw Randy heading our way and slid a little lower, wishing we didn't share the same bus.

"Found it!" Nixon pulled a glossy brochure from his backpack. He held it in front of my nose. "You have to read this."

It was too close to my face for me to read anything. "What is it?"

"Camp Awonjahela!"

"Awonja-whatcha?"

"A-won-ja-he-la," he repeated more slowly. "It's an old Indian word that means friendship."

"What the heck is it?"

"It's a summer camp," said Nixon. "Marcy went last year. She had the best time. I get to go this year, and my parents thought it would be more fun if I went with a friend." He looked at me, eyebrows raised expectantly. "What do you think?"

"About what?"

"Do you want to come with me?"

I looked down at the brochure. A picture of a sailboat on a lake was splashed across the front.

"I'll take that," a voice said, snatching the paper from my hands.

"Hey!" I yelled. Randy walked to the back of the bus, the camp brochure held over his head like a trophy. My brother was always stealing things from me.

"That's mine," called Nixon.

"I'll get it for you, Nix," said Marcy, following Randy down the aisle. "Don't worry."

"Thanks." Nixon sighed, turning back into his seat.

"Sorry," I said. It wasn't easy being my best friend. I was always apologizing for Randy's behavior. I often wondered what it would be like to have a nice sister like Marcy. She and Randy had been dating off and on the last few months. It was off and on because it usually only took a few weeks for Randy to do something really stupid that made Marcy come to her senses for a while. Why she kept making up with him was beyond me since Marcy seems like a really smart girl. I figure Randy must be one of the luckiest guys around to get so many chances. If I were Marcy, I would have dumped him for good a long time ago.

"I guess you'll just have to tell me about the camp," I said.

Nixon's face brightened. "It'll be great, Harry. It's six days in the Adirondack mountains, and they have a big lake, boats, campouts, archery, even a rifle range."

I'd never tried to shoot a bow and arrow, or a rifle, but both sounded cool. I'd also never been away from home for a whole week before. Sure, I'd slept over at Nixon's house a bunch of times, but that's just down the street. If anything ever went wrong, I could walk back home. But at camp, a lot of things could happen and I would be stuck there. I could get sick, or there might be a tornado, or what if I woke up in the middle of the night and didn't remember where I was?

Who knows, maybe I'm just paranoid from living with Randy for all these years. But in my opinion it's always good to think through what might go wrong so you can be prepared. That's what my teacher always says we should do, although I don't know if she is talking about sleepovers.

The more Nixon told me about the camp, however, the less I worried about sleeping away from home. As soon as I got off the bus, I ran home to ask my mom.

"So, can I go?" I asked, after I'd shared the details.

"Are you sure you can handle that, Frog Legs?" said Randy from the other side of the kitchen.

I hated it when he called me that name, but I'd pretty much stopped arguing about it. When you have a brother like Randy, you have to choose your battles.

"Randy, what have I told you about calling your brother that name?" Mom scolded.

Randy just chuckled, his usual, sinister grin on his face.

"I'll have to ask your father," said Mom. "He gets home on Wednesday."

Like usual, Dad was away on a business trip. This time he was in Milwaukee, which I think is in Wisconsin, or maybe Michigan. I'm not sure.

"Can't we just call him?" I asked. I've never been to Milwaukee, but I'm pretty sure Dad's phone should still work there. It's not like one of those faraway places where you have to get special cell service.

"Summer camp is expensive, Harry."

"But it sounds really fun," I whined.

"I agree," said Mom, "but we want to make sure he's in the right frame of mind to say yes. It's better to ask in person."

"Nixon's parents are letting him go," I said, flopping down into the kitchen chair as Mom chopped a carrot. "In fact, they're paying double since Nixon and Marcy are both going."

Randy's ears perked up at Marcy's name. "You know, Mom, Harry showed me the brochure on the bus. Maybe I could go too."

"I didn't show you the brochure, jerk," I answered. "You took it."

"Harry, don't say jerk," said Mom.

Randy's eyes drifted to the window that faced Marcy's house. "If I went, I could help keep an eye on him; make sure he doesn't get homesick and all."

"I don't need you to babysit me," I said, frowning. It was so annoying how Randy tried to make himself sound like *Brother of the Year*.

Worst Brother of the Year was more like it.

"I'll discuss it with your father," said Mom as she turned on the stove. "Now get upstairs and start your homework and let me get dinner started." She looked up slyly. "Unless one of you wants to help out…"

"That's okay," we both answered together. That was one thing both Randy and I could agree on.

CABIN ELEVEN: CHAPTER TWO

Dad said yes to Camp Awonjahela. That's the good news. The bad news was that he said Randy could come too.

A week at camp sounded awesome, but I knew all too well how much tormenting my brother could squeeze into a week when we were out of our parents' view. Would I have even asked to go to camp if I had known Randy would be there too?

Apparently, it helped that Camp Awonjahela has a scholarship program for families with more than one kid. You always hear people say that money isn't the most important thing. I agree, but whoever said that probably also had a lot of money. If we were rich, Dad might not be away working all the time. Then, instead of Camp Awonjahela, we could go camping together at the state park, just him and me. That probably wouldn't work either, since I'm sure Randy would have to come too, but I could dream.

So once Dad said yes, Mom went ahead and registered us for one week at the camp. They gave us a list of everything we needed to bring with us. She sent me to gather my clothes and supplies a week ahead of time so I wouldn't wait until the last minute to pack.

Personally, I think doing things at the last minute is a much more efficient use of time. But Mom says it just creates unnecessary anxiety. Living with Randy, I know all about anxiety, so I decided not to argue with her about it. I try to help her out with things like that when I can. I figure if Randy was my kid, I'd need a break wherever I could get one.

The list said electronics of any kind (including phones, video game players, headphones, and anything like that) were prohibited. That didn't sound fair to me. But Randy would probably have an even harder time managing without electronics for a week. Mom said we'd both have to cope. I guess the camp wants us to get closer to nature and smell the roses. When I thought of that, I reminded Randy to make sure he brought deodorant or else everyone would smell more than the roses, if you know what I mean. He told me to shut up.

I opened my dresser drawer and read the packing

list aloud. "Seven pairs of underwear, seven pairs of socks, swimsuit, extra sneakers, beach towel, bath towel, long pants, sweatshirt." I guess the last two were in case it got cold. "Poncho, shorts, seven t-shirts, toothbrush, toothpaste, shampoo, bar of soap, sunscreen, bug spray, water bottle or canteen, sleeping bag, pillow."

Geesh. That was a lot of stuff. I might have to rent a truck just to carry everything. Later that week, I took the giant duffel bag from the attic and managed to stuff everything in. With my sleeping bag and pillow under one arm and the enormous duffel over the other shoulder, I could barely walk. Randy called me a wimp and said he could carry both of ours no problem, but there was no way I was letting him near my stuff. He'd probably check it into the girls' side of camp or throw it in the lake.

The bus for camp left from the parking lot at the county library. Dad was on another business trip, in Tallahassee this time I think, but he told us over the phone to listen to the counselors and to stay out of poison ivy. He made Randy promise to be nice to me. Randy promised, but I'm pretty sure he had his fingers crossed.

Mom seemed kind of weepy to see us go. She kept giving us instructions even as we waited to board the bus.

"Behave yourselves. And don't forget to brush your teeth. Be careful in the lake. Don't go out too deep. Harry, try to make some new friends. Randy, don't torment your brother."

It seemed like she was going to repeat everything she'd ever told us before we could leave. Randy finally gave her a hug and stepped on the bus. I felt nervous again. But it was too late to back out now. I gave her one last wave, and then I followed Randy onto the bus.

CABIN ELEVEN: CHAPTER THREE

The bus to Camp Awonjahela was a lot like the one that took us to school. I sat right next to Nixon. Randy and Marcy were in the back with the older kids. It was a six-hour ride into the mountains to reach camp, but at least we were not going school. I shuddered at the thought that my schoolteachers might actually be waiting for me at camp, ready to pass out math worksheets. That would be hideous.

Marcy and some of the older girls who had been to camp before were leading the back of the bus in a singalong. They were singing a silly song about ants marching through the woods. I looked around the rows at the smiling faces and people singing. Mom likes to say that Randy and I are more inventive and play better together when we don't have our electronics to fool with. Maybe that applies to everyone.

"What are you looking forward to most?" asked Nixon.

"I don't know." I thought for a moment. "Maybe the lake?"

Nixon nodded. "Yeah, that will be fun. Marcy says there are lots of games and competitions, too."

"Competitions?" I hadn't heard that. I glanced at Randy in the back of the bus. Most competitions in my house ended up with me in severe pain.

"Yeah," answered Nixon. "The cabins compete against each other in games like tug of war and swimming races. There's even a huge game of capture the flag."

"Cool." Those did sound fun. Maybe if they kept my cabin away from Randy's, the week might be okay.

"Hey!" a shout came from the back of the bus. I turned around to see Marcy stand up quickly and glare at Randy.

I shook my head. Like I said, it was only a matter of time until my brother did something stupid. She marched up the aisle to the front. I don't think you're really supposed to move around like that when the bus is moving, but Mr. Early didn't seem to notice.

Mr. Early was a retired school bus driver who still helped out with driving for summer camps and church groups. He was kind of old. I think Mom raised an eyebrow when she saw he was driving. You'd think with a last name like Early, he'd always be on time, but Mr. Early was always late. I think that's why he stopped driving kids to school, but Nixon says he got fired.

Marcy sat down in the first row on the right side. She's always super easy to talk to, so not surprisingly, she quickly started chatting with Mr. Early. Nixon told me she volunteers once a month at the Sleepy Pines Nursing Home down the road and reads to the old people who are stuck in their beds. You'd never catch me doing that, but I guess it's pretty nice. Randy was still at the back of the bus talking to Cole Bradley, but he kept staring up front at Marcy.

"Did you know there are three thousand lakes in the Adirondack region of New York State?" said Nixon.

"Uh, huh." I nodded, half listening. Nixon was always coming up with interesting facts like that. Well, at least he thought they were interesting. I think he'd memorized the hundred *National Geographic Fun Fact* books that he'd checked out from the library over the school year. Maybe someday he could be on a game show like *Jeopardy*.

"Yep. There are also three kinds of venomous snakes and more than six thousand black bears."

Bears? I turned and looked him in the eyes. "Really?"

"That's right, and—"

Before Nixon could finish, a shoulder banged into my head from the aisle. "Ouch!" I groaned, looking up.

"Oh, sorry about that, Frog Legs," said Randy, grinning. He continued past our row and sat next to Marcy in the front.

"She's not going to like that," muttered Nixon, watching his sister turn her head toward the window each time Randy tried to talk to her.

I had been asking Nixon for ages if he knew why Marcy put up with Randy in the first place, but he didn't know either. The best we could come up with was she felt sorry for him and liked to help people in need, kind of like the old people in the nursing home. Randy was definitely in need. In need of a new personality.

Marcy still wasn't talking to him, which I knew would make Randy mad. I sunk lower in my seat since when Randy got mad he usually took it out on me. But instead of marching back down the aisle, he stepped into the stairwell by the door of the bus to try and look Marcy in the face.

I know for a fact you're not allowed to stand in the stairwell. Especially when the bus is moving. That's probably even against the law. Maybe if we got pulled over, Randy would be sent to jail.

"Get back to your seat, mister!" Mr. Early yelled. But Randy wasn't listening. He was pleading with Marcy to talk to him, but she kept shaking her head.

"What's he doing?" asked Nixon. "That's not safe."

I nodded in agreement as Mr. Early yelled louder. "Hey, mister! I said, sit down!" Mr. Early was paying more attention to Randy than he was the road.

Randy finally stepped up out of the stairwell, but he accidentally bumped into the door handle. The front door folded back, a gust of air pouring through the seats. Now everyone was watching. Kids were yelling. The wind was howling. And we were still barreling along the freeway.

Mr. Early lunged to shut the door.

"Watch out!" screamed Marcy.

A tractor-trailer horn blared. The bus had drifted across the lane toward the median and the oncoming traffic!

BROTHER WARS: CABIN ELEVEN

Ten-year-old Harry can't wait for a week of summer camp in the mountains at Camp Awonjahela. Unfortunately, his older brother Randy is coming too. If that weren't bad enough, his Cabin Eleven is cursed. Or at least that's the legend. Even worse, a girl named Poison Ivy won't stop talking to him. No one from Cabin Eleven has ever won the camp-wide competition, but that's exactly what Harry and his friends set out to do. To break the curse, they'll have to survive the overnight hike, win Capture the Flag, and face the mysterious figure who lives across the lake. But Randy isn't going to make it easy. When disaster strikes, this might be one brother war too many for Harry.

AVAILABLE IN HARDCOVER, PAPERBACK AND EBOOK VERSIONS.

ABOUT THE AUTHOR

Steven K. Smith is the author of *The Virginia Mysteries* and *Brother Wars* series for middle grade readers, as well as the parenting memoir, *Splashing in the Deep End: Adventures Raising Boys.* He lives with his wife, three sons, and a golden retriever named Charlie, in Richmond, Virginia.

For more information:

www.VirginiaMysteries.com

steve@myboys3.com

ALSO BY STEVEN K. SMITH

The Virginia Mysteries:

Summer of the Woods

Mystery on Church Hill

Ghosts of Belle Isle

Secret of the Staircase

Midnight at the Mansion

Shadows at Jamestown

Brother Wars

Brother Wars: Cabin Eleven

Splashing in the Deep End

(parenting non-fiction)

DID YOU ENJOY BROTHER WARS?

Would You ... Review?

Online reviews are crucial for indie authors like me. They help bring credibility and make books more discoverable by new readers. No matter where you purchased your book, if you could take a few moments and give an honest review at one of the following websites, I'd be so grateful.

Amazon.com
BarnesandNoble.com
Goodreads.com

Thank you and thanks for reading!

Steve

68272537R00080

Made in the USA
Middletown, DE
15 September 2019